FIRE DRILL

Paul DuBois Jacobs and **Jennifer Swender**

illustrated by **Huy Voun Lee**

HENRY HOLT AND COMPANY • NEW YORK

Louisburg Library
Bringing People and Information Together

Henry Holt and Company, LLC, *Publishers since 1866*
175 Fifth Avenue, New York, New York 10010
www.HenryHoltKids.com

Henry Holt® is a registered trademark of Henry Holt and Company, LLC.
Text copyright © 2010 by Jacobs and Swender, Inc.
Illustrations copyright © 2010 by Huy Voun Lee
All rights reserved.
Distributed in Canada by H. B. Fenn and Company Ltd.

Library of Congress Cataloging-in-Publication Data
Jacobs, Paul DuBois.
Fire drill / Paul DuBois Jacobs and Jennifer Swender ; illustrated by Huy Voun Lee. — 1st ed.
p.   cm.
Summary: In this story told in brief rhyming text, students
in a class follow the proper procedures during a fire drill.
ISBN 978-0-8050-8953-0
[1. Fire drills—Fiction. 2. Safety—Fiction. 3. Schools—Fiction.]
I. Swender, Jennifer. II. Lee, Huy Voun, ill. III. Title.
PZ8.3.J1383Fi 2010   [E]—dc22   2009005268

First Edition—2010 / Designed by April Ward
The artist used cut-paper collage to create the illustrations for this book.
Printed in October 2009 in China by Leo Paper, Heshan City,
Guangdong Province, on acid-free paper. ∞

1 3 5 7 9 10 8 6 4 2

For Natalia and Nicolao
—P. D. J. and J. S.

For Seiji Ikuta
—H. V. L.

FIRE DRILL RULES
1. Be quiet. Listen to the teache
2. Follow directions.
3. Get in line.
4. Walk. Don't run.
5. Wait until teacher says GO.
6. Get a hug.

What a day!

We read. We play.

We paint.
We sing.

Then loud bells ring.

Look up. Be still.
This is a fire drill.

Put down toys.
Get in line.

Here we go.
Take your time.

EXIT

FIRE DRILL RULES
Be quiet. Listen to the teacher.
Follow directions.
Get in line.
Walk. Do not run.
Wait ____ ther sa
et

Watch the teacher.
Walk. Walk. Walk.

Out the door.
Down the stairs.
Stay in line.
Stay in pairs.

Stop right there.
Find your place.

Do not climb.
Do not chase.

Hear your name.
Raise your hand.
Say out loud:
"Here I am!"

Now we wait.
Now we stay.

Until the teacher says, "Okay!"

Up the stairs.
In the door.
The teacher counts,
1, 2, 3, 4 . . .

Take your place
on the rug.
Get a sticker.
Get a hug.

That was fun.
What a thrill!
We're all done.